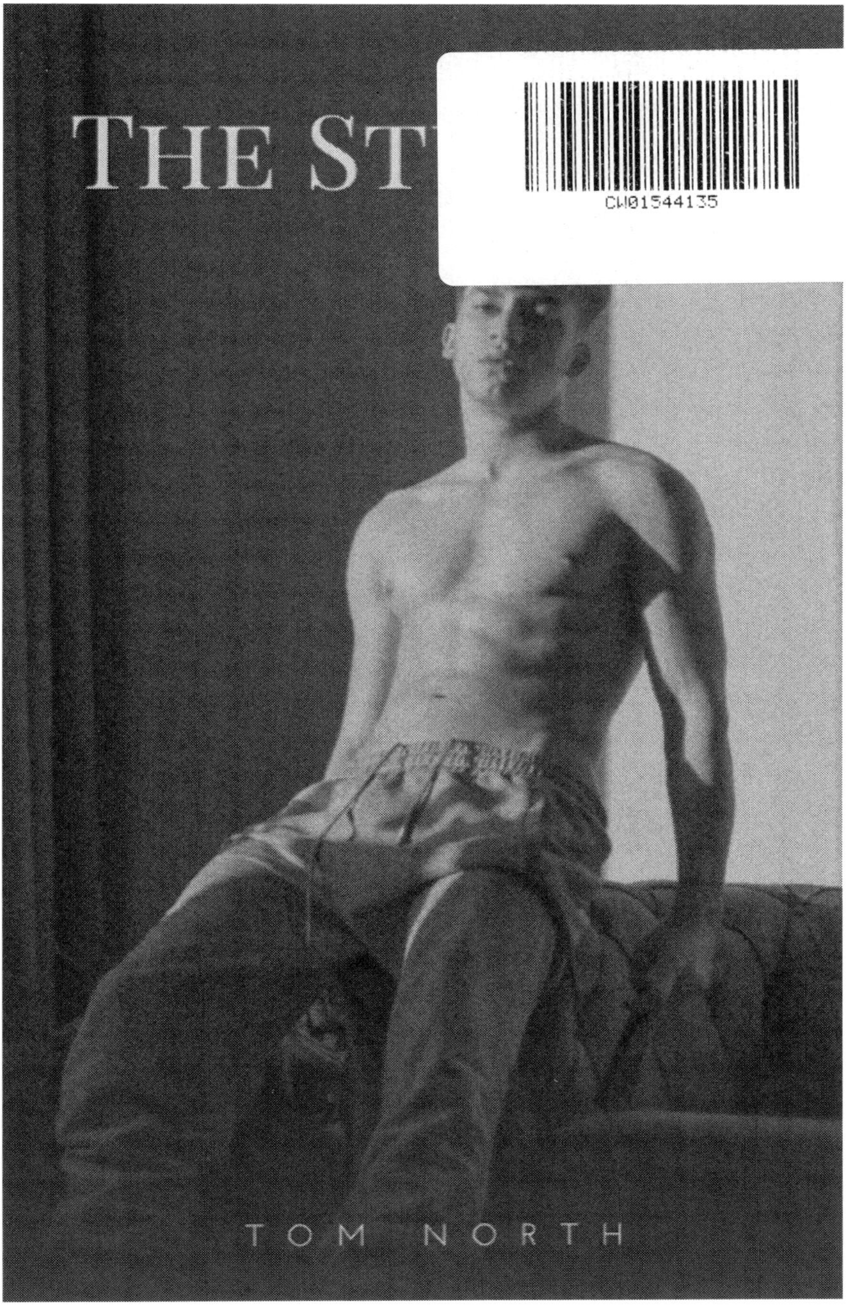

THE ST

T O M N O R T H

Chapter One

It's was David's first day in his dorms at college. The day he'd been waiting for. He had been desperate to escape his hometown and finally get some independence. To finally work out who he was and what he wanted from his life.

To finally move out into the world where people didn't know him as the son of a cop, where he didn't have to watch his every move in case his Dad would disapprove. And he did it. He was finally free of his parents and their watchful eyes.

David was in his new room, carefully packing away all of his belonging, finding just the right place for everything. He put his underwear neatly into his top draw, tucking a packet of condoms in the corner - dreaming that he'd find a moment to use them before too long. He was still a virgin. But hopefully not for too much longer.

He moved on to his bookshelf, pulling out several novels from different genres. A collection of fiction he'd read over and over again, until he'd memorised it like an old friend. He set these aside, along with some other older books he'd collected over the years.

He finished up and then made his way to the mirror. Observing himself in his new space. His brown hair looked reasonably tidy, a slight fringe tickling his forehead. Brown eyes looking full of hope.

His phone chimed softly from his bag, pulling him from his thoughts. He grabbed his phone, opening his messages quickly. A single message from 'Hey, you ignoring me?', followed by several missed calls from his best friend, Shawn.

Chuckling to himself while sending back a quick reply, he placed his phone back in his pocket, turning to face the rest of his belongings. His eyes lingered upon the bookshelf. There was a lot of knowledge stored in there. Knowledge about life, freedom, love. Books about self discovery, about life outside of your parent's expectations. The book were his only escape from the monotony of life back home. But now he was free, he could explore all the things he'd only ever read about. One big thing those books couldn't show him - and the only thing he really cared about right now - was what it would actually feel like to fall in love with someone, to have sex with someone. To feel someone else's body inside your own. He turned himself on just thinking about it, feeling the erection grow in his pants.

The door swung open and David's new roommate walked into the room. He was tall, probably 6 feet if David had to guess. His skin was a shade darker than David's. Black curly hair sticking out in every direction. Blue eyes scanning the room before landing on the boy in front of him. The boy he had just met. The boy he was going to spend every night sleeping beside, sharing dreams and secrets.

"Hey man," He said, moving forward toward David. The man casually threw his arms around David pulling him into a hug, "It's nice to you" He had the biggest most genuine smile David had ever seen, and he seemed to be so relaxed. His muscles moving with an ease and masculinity that made David feel even hornier. He suddenly became very aware of his erection.

"Yeah I'm David…I uh…" He managed to say, still

trying to pull away from the man's strong grip.

The guy smiled and gave David one last squeeze before stepping back.

"Nice to meet you," He replied, making his way over to his bed. Sitting down and resting his head on the soft mattress. "My name is Liam." He stretched his legs out in front of him, reaching into his hoodie pocket, pulling out a pack of cigarettes. He pulled one out, lighting it, taking a drag and blowing out the smoke gracefully. "So how are you liking the school so far?"

David nodded, sitting down on his own bed, covering his crotch with his hands "It's okay," He paused, unsure of whether to go on, "I mean I didn't expect anything less but I am kinda nervous.."

Liam chuckled lightly, "You'll do fine, don't worry about it. What classes you're interested in?" He asked, taking another drag on his cigarette.

David shrugged, "Um…History, I think I'd like to major in that. I'm good at languages though." He replied.

"Well I'm sure you can make it through," Liam

grinned, "So listen, I know we've only just met, but, sharing a room together for the whole year we should probably come up with some ground rules."

"Ground rules?"

"Yeah, just so we can agree on what we can and can't do in the space. Like girls for instance."

"Girls?"

"Yeah, girls dummy, what do we do if either of us wants to bring a girl back? I don't wanna have to kick you out. But if you're gonna be weird about me having sex in front of you."

"Sex?!" David almost shouted, dropping his hands from his crotch, his ears starting to turn pink. "What are you talking about?"

"Are you deaf? You know like…sex. With a girl," Liam replied, "Do you mind if I bring girls back? I don't want to waste my first year on campus."

David shook his head and sighed, "No no, I don't mind. You can bring whoever you want back."

Liam smiled brightly, lighting another cigarette, "Alright then, I'll let you settle in here then. I have to go talk to a few other guys so they can give me a tour."

As Liam stood up and started walking past David he reached out and took Liam's hand. Their fingers interlocked and Liam leaned in close and whispered, "Is that a boner in your pants?"

Then, he pulled back, laughed and headed towards the door. "See ya later David," He waved over his shoulder.

David was left alone in the room blood rushing to his cheeks in embarrassment, a little bit taken aback by the conversation, he was turned on a disappointed all at the same time. This Liam guy was really hot and he was going to be having sex in the room next to him. This is not exactly the fantasy he had in mind. His cock was still pulsing in his pants and currently he only had one solution.

Chapter Two

David had been at the College for three weeks now and he still had not managed to lose his virginity. It turned out that finding a guy to sleep with in this place was harder than he thought. And it didn't help that David was terrified of bringing a guy back to his dorm to sleep with. He didn't want Liam to be watching him while he was fucked for the first time. He didn't even know if Liam would be okay with him being gay. They hadn't spoken about it at all. In fact, they had barely spoken. Every time Liam was in the room David just choked up, his penis hardening in an instant. He couldn't stop his body from craving Liam

It was late on Friday evening and David was on his own in the room. Liam had gone out to a party somewhere. David was on his phone, scrolling through a hook-app he had downloaded but not had the confidence to use yet. The App was pretty uninspiring, just a sea on men's chests. David desperately wanted to have sex, but he wanted to know the person he was going to do it with.

'Hey' - the word popped up on his screen. David's heart skipped a beat, he tapped on the profile photo of the person who sent the message. He couldn't see their whole face, just the most gorgeous smile.

'Hey' David responded.

'How are you doing?'

'I'm okay - just a bit bored.'

'Hopefully I can entertain you.'

David laughed at the response and typed 'Oh yeah?' He wasn't expecting anything special.

'Mmhmm. So what are you up to?'

'I'm just hanging out in my room.'

'Cool, what do you have planned for the weekend?'

'I dunno..probably watch a movie or something..' David admitted sheepishly, biting his lip.

'That sounds like fun!'

"What about you? You must have loads of options right?'

'Hmm....actually not really..maybe we could maybe, do something?'

David hesitated, not knowing how to respond. Then his phone vibrated again. The guy had sent through a picture showing the rest of his face. He was absolutely gorgeous, high cheek bones, amazing smile.

'I'm Tim'

'I'm David' David sent through a pic of himself.

'You're cute, wanna hang out? I'm free now.'

'What did you want to do?'

'Well, let's not spoil the suspense.'

David began shaking, his cock again hardening at the thought of what he might do with this man. His dick started throbbing in his pants as he tried to fight against the growing erection in his pants. He could already imagine this Tim dude touching his naked body, kissing and sucking down his neck, touching places that made him moan. David was practically drooling by now, his hands were trembling against his phone.

'Yeah, I definitely want to see what we can do.'

'Great. Can I come to yours?'

David looked over at Liam's empty bed. He probably wouldn't be back until the early hours of the morning.

'Sure.' David sent through his address and waited

patiently for the mystery man to arrive. About twenty minutes passed by before there was a knock at the door. He jumped off the bed, rushing across the room opening the door to reveal Tim standing outside.

He stepped inside the room closing the door behind him. He was even more gorgeous in person. Tall and chiselled with muscles bulging through his jacket. His hair was black and wavy. His skin was tan, which contrasted nicely with the dark blue eyes.

Tim walked closer to David, stopping in front of him, their faces inches apart. "Hi" He smiled looking up into David's bright green eyes.

"Hi," David said, swallowing harshly.

A small smirk appeared on Tim's face and he placed a gentle finger under David's chin and lifted it up slightly, placing a quick kiss on David's lips. David let out a small hum of approval, his breathing becoming quicker.

Tim took a step back, letting David look at him. He looked over at David's chest, looking down at his hard member. He smirked and slowly reached out his hand. Taking the hem of David's shirt and pulling it over his head. He tossed it onto the floor. A second later, Tim's hands were wrapped around David's waist, pushing him onto the bed. He pulled David closer and pressed his lips against David's, his tongue sliding inside his mouth. David let out a small gasp as he felt Tim's hand move down his stomach, slipping underneath his sweatpants.

He moaned quietly when Tim brushed his fingers lightly against his dick. Slowly moving his hand up and down, making soft circular movements against his tip. This was happening so fast.

"Fuck." He mumbled, pushing his hips forward, allowing himself to get lost in the feeling of the warm touch of Tim's fingertips.

Tickling and brushing his thumb along the tip of David's erection, making it twitch slightly under his touch. Tim moved his hand up a fraction, tracing along David's shaft. His eyes widening at the sight of the hardened tip, his own cock twitching in anticipation.

"Fuck," He repeated lowly, pulling away briefly to look up into David's eyes.

He smiled softly before pulling his hand back to caress David's length again. David tilted his head back into the mattress as he let out quiet whines, his body tensing, wanting nothing more than to feel Tim's hands stroking the length of his cock.

"Come on," He murmured, tugging at the bottom of David's underwear with a single hand. "Let me have you."

David nodded eagerly, pulling his sweatpants down as quickly as possible.

David lay half naked while Tim was fully clothed, taking in the sight of David's cock. Then he leant down and took David's cock in his mouth. David gasped loudly at the sudden sensation of Tim's mouth engulfing his cock in a vice grip.

His fingers dug into the sheets tightly, his nails leaving crescent shaped impressions in them as he bit down onto his bottom lip nervously.

"Fuck, Tim, please….fuck…" David moaned, grinding his hips into mattress, trying to keep up with Tim's ministrations.

The feeling of teeth gently grazing the underside of

his cock set it off. David gasped loudly and thrust his hips upward, digging his fingers into the sheets again.

"Shit! Shit! Fuck! More Tim!" He begged, his voice raspy from his desire.

Tim's hands gripped the base of David's cock as he sucked hungrily at it, licking and sucking every last drop of precum from it, earning a loud moan from David.

"Fuck! Tim! Fuck me, fuck me! Fuck!" David shouted, gripping the sheets even tighter.

He slid a hand around David's balls squeezing them gently. He continued to stroke David.

David could feel himself getting close. He had never felt so good in his entire life. He couldn't believe he was finally getting sucked off. It was a dream come true. Tim was just bringing his hands down to David's arsehole when the door to the room flung open and Liam walked in, stumbling and drunk. Liam froze staring at the two men while Time jumped up, wiping his mouth and looking horrified.

David panicked and covered his cock with his hands.

"Liam…" David stuttered, hoping he would understand what was happening without having to say it explicitly.

"I should go." Tim said and ran out of the door without making eye contact with either of the two guys.

Liam still said nothing as David lay there covering his half erect cock. Liam shut the door behind him and stumbled over to his bed. David could feel his cheeks turning red again. He was mortified.

David pulled his sweatpants back on and slid into bed. Awkard silence drowning the room. He lay there for ages wondering if Liam would say anything. But he didn't. After about 10 minutes he had passed out. It took David hours to get to sleep, but eventually his thoughts settled and his eyes closed.

Chapter Three

The next day David was sitting in a History lecture, trying to focus on the events leading up to World War II. But all he could really think about was last night and how embarrassed he felt at Liam walking in on him getting sucked off.

Liam still hadn't said a word to him about it. When David left that morning Liam was still laying in bed with a hangover.

"What's wrong with you this morning?" Shawn said, sitting next to him. Shawn and David had been best friends since childhood and had agreed to escape to the same college together.

"I'm fine."

"Bullshit. I know that look. Something has happened. What is it?"

"Honeslty. It's nothing."

"Tell me."

"It's Nothing." David huffed, pretending to focus on note taking. "Just leave it alone."

He didn't tell Shawn about what happened last

night, he wanted to deal with this by himself. But Shawn wasn't going to let him be.

"Are you sure? Because something clearly isn't okay with you. You've been acting weird ever since you got here this morning. And don't act like you aren't thinking about him too."

"Who?"

"Your new roommate. I know you have the hots for him." Shawn giggled, punching David in the arm.

"Jesus Christ Shawn. Will you stop it?"

"Alright, listen. I'll leave it. Just be careful. You don't want to get involved with your roommate. It would make things so weird if it went wrong."

"Nothing's gonna happen anyway. He's straight. It's just a stupid crush. I'll get over it." David scoffed, trying to brush it off as if it was no big deal.

The bell rang signalling the end of the class. David packed his bag and walked out.

"Hey listen. There's a party tonight, if you want to come?"

"I don't know."

"Come on. You can't sit stewing in your room

every night. Meet me at mine at 7 and we'll go together. I'll bring the beers."

David hesitated for a moment, then thought about the prospect of spending another evening on his own and having to engage with Liam after last night.

"Fine. I'll see you at yours."

"That's the spirit. We'll find you a nice man in no time." Shawn winked as he threw his bag over his shoulder and sauntered off. All David could think about was sex. Yet he was absolutely terrified of actually going out into the world and getting it. Getting close to someone who doesn't know him. The whole idea scared him. But at the same time he kind of craved it. A part of him craved that feeling of intimacy and warmth. He wanted to kiss and touch and feel everything with someone else.

A smile appeared on his face, remembering last night, Tim's mouth wrapped around his cock. Maybe that was worth all the effort.

***

David stared blankly at his wardrobe, not knowing what to wear. He'd just showered and wasn't sure how to best present himself at this party. At the bottom of the wardrobe was a jock strap that he had managed to get a hold of from the Internet, though he wasn't sure he'd ever be brave enough to wear it. The thought of wearing it turned him on so much it scared him. Was tonight the night? He wasn't sure. He decided against it.

He sighed, grabbing a shirt and a pair of jeans before going into the bathroom.

He changed into his clothes slowly, thinking about the party and what was going to happen once he got there. Would he meet anyone interesting? Or would he just end up talking about the weather or football? He shook his head slightly. This was ridiculous, he wasn't made for this. He thought it would be easy once he got to college, but it turns out he felt just as trapped as ever. Trapped by his own mind.

Before he knew it, it was quarter to seven and he was standing outside Shawn's dorm.

"Finally you made it." Shawn exclaimed, stepping forward to greet him. "You look great. Are you ready?"

"Yeah. Let's get this over with." David mumbled as he followed his best friend. They walked down the street laughing and chatting. Before they knew it they reached the party.

The music was blasting through the speakers in the living room and people were dancing crazily in the middle of it all. People were screaming, drinking and dancing.

"I'll go grab some drinks. You want anything?" Shawn asked, heading for the bar.

"Uh, yeah. Just whatever you're having." David replied as he watched his friend walk away. He looked around the room. It was mostly people he vaguely recognized. Some of them he knew. Others he didn't. They all seemed to be enjoying themselves though.

He spotted one guy standing near the stairs talking to someone. His hair was jet black and he had piercing blue eyes. David couldn't help but stare. The guy caught his eye and smiled, nodding at him.

"Your drink sir!" Shawn yelled jokingly.

David tore his eyes away from the guy and headed towards his friend. He grabbed a bottle of beer out of

Shawn's hands.

"Thanks." He mumbled.

"See it's not so bad! You're having fun. I can tell!"

The evening trickled on and David and Shawn got slowly drunk. Dancing away in the living room. Letting the bass of the speakers rumble in their chests. Every time they finish a glass of beer, they'd run straight for another. David could feel his inhibitions slipping.

"I need to piss." David shouted into Shawn's ear. "Ill be right back."

"Okay man. Don't get lost." Shawn shouted back.

"I won't." David grinned, rushing down the hallway and into the bathroom.

He locked the door behind him. He ran his hands over his messy curls and looked at himself in the mirror. The sight made him laugh. He looked like he had seen hell. Dark circles under his bloodshot eyes. His hair sticking up in all directions. He was drunk. Far more drunk than he thought he was. Maybe this College thing wasn't so bad, maybe he could actually manage to be normal and let himself go

He took a deep breath and tried to ignore his reflection. He walked back out into the living room to rejoin Shawn.

He saw the guy he had been staring at earlier standing in front of the window watching the party. Something in him flipped and he let his fear go. He walked up to the guy and cleared his throat.

"Um hi." He whispered shyly, unsure of himself, but feigning confidence.

"Hi." The stranger said. His voice swas deep. It sent a shiver down David's spine.

They both stood awkwardly. No one said anything. David kept scanning the room for a way to start a conversation with him. "Where are your friends?"

"They're around somewhere. It's pretty busy in here." He nodded toward the crowd in the living room.

"You having a nice evening?" David leaned against the wall. Feeling his confidence grow with every moment. This guy was gorgeous. David'a stomach was filling with sparks.

Every part of his body was drawn to him and he

found himself wanting nothing more than to get closer and touch him.

"Yep." He chuckled. "It's pretty crowded here. I was wondering if you wanted to go somewhere a bit quieter?" The alcohol was flooding David's brain. He felt alive.

"I'm okay thanks." The guy said with a wince

"Awwh, come on. I can show you a good time." David said as he stroked the guys arm.

"Get your hands off me, Faggot. I said no." The guy pushed David so hard that he fell on his ass in shock. People nearby stopped their conversations and looked at the scene before them.

"What the fuck is your problem!" David screamed back, anger coursing through his veins. He got up again and tried to punch him in the face.

The guy dodged his fist by turning around to grab his wrist. He twisted David's hand around behind his back and held it against his chest. David struggled to break free and pulled at his arm in to no avail.

"Let go of me!" David cried, struggling desperately to get away.

The guy laughed and let go of David's arm. He punched David across the face, causing him to stumble backwards, holding his nose.

Everyone started shouting at the commotion. David panicked and tried to scramble to the door. He just wanted to get away. To run and hide from all these people, staring. He stumbled through the mass of people, knocking over two of them on the way. He reached the entrance of the house, pushing through the crowds. He broke through the doors and sprinted down the street.

As he ran, he felt the shame crush down on him.

Chapter Four

David's head was pounding. His mouth was dry. He felt nauseous and his nose was swollen and sore. He was laying in his bed, completely naked, his bare ass hanging out, his cock somehow hard as a rock. Tears streamed down his cheeks and his heart hammered wildly in his chest. He couldn't remember a single thing from last night. He could barely open his eyes. Everything hurt. The pain felt sharp and immediate. As his mind began to clear he realized what had happened to him.

He sat up suddenly, letting the covers fall as his cock bounced out into the open air. His head screaming in pain.

"Nice night?" he head a voice say.

He looked over at the bed opposite his. Squinting his eyes, trying to bring the person into focus. It was Liam. Liam was sitting up in bed, leaning forward, looking at David with a curious expression on his face.

David groaned, dropping back down onto his pillow as his head began to swim again.

Liam frowned concerned. "Are you okay?" He asked, concern lacing his words.

"Yes.. I think so..." He answered quietly, closing his eyes to try and stop the pounding pain in his head.

"Well you can't feel too bad. You've got a massive boner still. Does that thing ever go away?" Liam nodded towards David's throbbing cock.

"Oh Shit." David squirmed, hiding himself in the covers.

"Why are you hiding? I've seen it all before. I mean I'm hot dude, but you don't have to have a boner every time I'm in the room." Liam laughed as he got out of bed, looking at the bulge of David's erection through the covers. "Wow. Good job. You must really love me then." Liam teased. "But don't worry. I've got you covered." He smirked, grabbing a pair of boxers and throwing them at David. "Put those on so we can have a little talk."

David reluctantly got out of bed, pulling on his boxers.

"What did you wanna talk about?" he asked hesitantly.

Liam sat at the end of his bed. "So… you are gay right?" Liam asked.

"Huh? What?" David replied, confused.

"You know. Like, you're interested in guys? Or did that guy the other night just trip and fall onto your dick?" Liam raised an eyebrow at him questioningly.

"I don't… I don't know." David replied.

"I don't mind dude. Just wasn't expecting to walk in on it."

David didn't know what to say. He had never been so embarrassed in his entire life and his face was throbbing in pain.

"What happened to you last night?" Liam asked. He moved closer to David.

"Uh…" David stuttered, trying to form some sort of answer. He looked everywhere except the boy.

"Come on David. You look pretty beat up. What happened?"

"It was nothing."

"You really like to keep people at a distance huh? Well okay, if that's what you want." Liam pushed himself up on his knee and walked back over to his side of the room. He grabbed his jacket from his closet and slipped it on. "Whatever you say. If you change your mind…" he shrugged. "You know where to find me." He walked past David and opened the door. He paused and turned around to look at David once more. Then he left.

David watched him leave with a heavy feeling in his gut.

No matter how many questions flooded his brain, he was too tired to figure any of it out. He laid back down and closed his eyes. The darkness consumed him and he drifted off to sleep.

* * *

He spent the next few days feeling sorry for himself in his room. Waiting for his face and his pride to heal. He had been ignoring Shawn's texts and only barely talking to Liam when he came into the room.

Late one evening he was laying in his bed, staring at the wall. He was wondering why on Earth he even came to college? Did he really think that he would suddenly get all the things that he wanted? He was a loser, there was no point even trying. He should just pack up and go back to his old life.

He was drifting in and out of consciousness when he heard giggling coming from the hallway. Then he heard the rumble of Liam's voice followed by some more giggles. The door to his room began to turn and slowly creak open.

"Ssssh, see, I told you he'd be sleeping. He won't event notice." Liam said.

"I don't know. It feels a bit weird to do it in front of him." The girl responded.

"It's fine. We have a deal." Liam grabbed the girl into a kiss and pulled her through the doorway, pushing her down on the bed.

David just lay there, listening to the sounds of clothes dropping to floor and skin rubbing together. He could hear them kissing and groaning.

He was so furious he could barely even move. But that didn't stop him from getting hard yet again at the thought of Liam naked and having sex in the same room as him. He just wished it was him that Liam had his cock inside.

David couldn't help but roll over so he could see what was happening. It was dark, there was only a slit of light coming in though the curtain from the streetlight. Enough to light up part of Liam's face as he thrust into the girl, leaning over her. She was moaning quietly as Liam grunted with every thrust.

David was rock hard and raging with jealousy. He had never felt so small. Liam turned his head suddenly and caught David's eye. They held eye contact for a few moments as Liam continued thrusting his cock into the girl. Then a grin came onto Liam's face and he winked at David. With that his thrusting became faster. He kept his eyes on David as he thrust harder and faster, letting his groaning get louder.

David couldn't help but start to stroke himself under the covers. Just gently, so Liam couldn't tell what he was doing.

They still kept eye contact with each other until Liam started to reach his climax. His grunting reached a fever pitch and his eyes shut closed in pleasure as he gave a few more violent thrusts before grunting and rolling off of the girl.

David stopped stroking. Feeling disgusted, turned on and embarrassed all at the same time. The pair opposite him seemed to drift into a gentle sleep after pulling the covers over themselves while David lay staring at the ceiling until finally the shame sent him into the oblivion of sleep.

Chapter Five

"What the hell is going on with you?" Shawn asked. Shawn had managed to drag David out of his room and out for a walk in the park. The two were walking slowly, taking in the cool winter morning. David didn't respond, he just stared sheepishly at his feet.

"You can't keep treating everyone like this David. You won't talk to me about anything. How am I supposed to help you if you won't let me in? I'm supposed to be your friend. I tell you absolutely everything that goes on in my life and to be honest it's kinda pissing me off that you just constantly shut me out. I was so worried about you after the other night. And you still won't talk to me about what happened. It's fucked up man."

"I'm sorry Shawn. I just don't want to talk about it."

"Is this about your roommate. What's his name? Liam?"

David didn't respond, but his cheeks immediately went bright red.

"Well I'm taking your silence as a yes. It's okay to have a crush on people you know."

"That's easy for you to say, straight boy." David snapped, half playfully.

"So that's what this is about. You feeling sorry for yourself just cause you're gay?"

"Not just because of that. It's just this whole time since being at college. Honestly it's been shit. Nothing has been like I thought it would be. I just had this idea in my head that I'd get here and suddenly live the life I wanted to live. That I'd meet loads of gorgeous guys and have amazing sex. But it's just all gone wrong. The only guys I meet are straight and have no interest and the one time I nearly got some action it was ruined because I'm sharing a room. It's all fucked up. I'm thinking I should just give up and go home. Especially after the other night at the party. How am I going to trust myself around other people ever again?"

David finished ranting and he stopped to catch his

breath.

Shawn remained silent for a few moments before responding.

"I don't think you will ever be able to trust yourself. Because you know you're a massive homo. I mean come on, have you seen you? You've been drooling over guys every chance you get! I've seen it!"

"Shut up Shawn!" David snapped defensively.

"But honestly dude, you gotta get it together." Shawn said sternly. "You know I support you no matter what right? You need to get rid of that fucking fear. So what you drool over guys? Own it! You're allowed to be attracted to people and want to fuck them."

David couldn't help but giggle slightly. Maybe it wasn't as bad as he thought it was.

"I had to listen to Liam screw some girl in our room last night." David said.

"Oh jeez! Now I understand why you look so pissed."

"It was horrible!" David's eyes sparked as he said it. Shawn studied his face for a moment.

"You liked it didn't you?"

David grinned ever so slightly.

"You fucking pervert." Shawn laughed as he hit his friend on the arm.

"Well, like you said. Nothing wrong with being attracted to people."

"Yeah, it's another thing to get your kicks out of your roommate fucking someone. But hey, who am I to judge? At least you've got access to a bit of action. I've had absolutely nothing."

They both laughed.

"It was a bit weird though." David continued, "While he was fucking her, I think he saw me watching. And he seemed to kinda of like that I was watching him. "

Shawn thought for a moment, then patted David on the shoulder, "Well buddy, maybe your straight roommate is not as straight as you think he is…"

***

Later that night David was working on an essay

his room. The light from his table lamp was pushing out a yellow glow. Liam was laying in his bed smoking a joint and staring at the ceiling. The two hadn't really spoken much, there was a strange tension in the air.

"Didn't keep you up last night did I?" Liam asked.

David carried on looking at his work and said, "No, it's fine."

Liam nodded and continued smoking his joint. A minute later David heard footsteps coming across the room. Liam was heading over in his direction. Then he felt a hand rest on his shoulder. "Sorry I interrupted your fun the other night."

"It's fine." David said.

"Whatever." Liam removed his hand from David's shoulder and continued smoking, staring casually at David's essay. Then he turned back to his bed and threw himself down onto it.

Then there was silence again.

"You gonna see that guy again?" Liam asked, "He seemed hot."

David's cheeks flushed and fire erupted in his stomach, "Probably not."

"That's a shame. It's nice for you to get some action. A few years ago I was just like you. Terrfied to even talk to a person. I get what it feels like."

"You don't know anything about how I feel." David snapped back.

"Sure" Liam replied.

"What's that supposed to mean?"

"Why are you so stressed tonight? Chill out man."

"I'm completely chilled out. Just because I don't have a joint hanging out my mouth doesn't mean I'm not relaxed."

"Yeah sure, you sound real relaxed."

"What is with you?" David turned around to face Liam.

"Absolutely nothing," Liam smirked.

"What did I do to deserve sharing a room with you? Can you just leave me alone please. I'm trying to do some work."

"Sure, if you want to keep pretending."

"Pretending about what?" David said slowly.

"I know you've got a thing for me. I've seen the way you look at me. I can feel the boner growing in your pants every time I'm in the room. I don't have a problem with it dude. In fact I'm kinda flattered, but there's no point pretending it doesn't exist. May as well face the reality. I'm a good looking guy, who can blame you?"

David kept silent. He didn't know what to say.

"Want me to fuck you?"

"Fuck off." David replied.

"I could bend you over that bed right now and fuck you raw. I've just had all my checks. C'mon, you know you'd like it." Liam gently grabbed his crotch.

"Leave me alone Liam, I'm not interested in you." David's cock was swelling in his underwear at the thought of it.

Liam moved over towards David and whispered in his ear, "You want my cock inside you. Don't you?" Liam grabbed David's erect cock and his breath tickled David's ear.

David gulped hard, felt a moment of hope and excitement and then he pushed Liam away, "Fuck you

Liam. I don't need this shit."

Liam chuckled and made his way back to his bed.

"Well, if you change your mind you know where I am." Liam went back to smoking his joint, leaning against the wall and gently resting his hand over his crotch.

David turned back to his essay in fury for a few moments and then ran out of the room to get some fresh air and escape the weird sexual tension in the room.

Chapter Six

"So you're telling me that he offered to fuck you there and then and you just ran away?" Shawn said in exasperation.

"He was just winding me up Shawn. He wasn't being serious. He was just teasing the gay boy to make himself feel better."

"How can you be sure about that?"

"I just know it. It's obvious. He was fucking a girl in front of me for Christ's sake."

"You never know these days" Shawn giggled as he returned to taking notes on the lecture.

A spark of hope kept threatening to take over in David's stomach. What if he really was offering to fuck him? The thought filled him so with so excitement he couldn't cope with it. The thought of them naked in their room, fucking like animals, sweating moaning, cumming all over each other. God David needed to get laid. And he needed it soon!

David and Shawn were making their way out of

the lecture hall when a familiar voice shouted in David's direction.

"Hey."

David turned to see a beautiful chiselled face staring back at him with a bashful smile spread across it.

"Hey." David replied awkwardly.

"I'll see you later. I've got to get to my next lecture." Shawn said as he left the two guys to chat.

"Sorry about the other night." David said. "I thought my roommate would be out all night. Didn't mean to ruin the mood."

"It's fine, don't worry about it. I've had worse embarrassing sexual encounters." Tim laughed, "Anyways before we were disturbed I was having a really great time." Tim leaned in closer and whispered, "Your cock tasted great."

David laughed, blushed and immediately got hard in the space of just a few moments.

"Well, im glad you liked it." he smiled.

"So, would you like to try again? I've got a free period now, if you're up for it?"

David's stomach sparked, the thought of having his cock sucked again had his blood pumping faster than ever.

"Sure." David blurted out.

"Great, where shall we go? I'd say come back to mine. But I don't live on campus. Might be a bit of a trek."

David considered his options. Liam should be out at lectures for the rest of the afternoon. But did he want to risk being caught in the act again? A small part of him was excited by the idea of Liam catching him with his cock getting sucked again. Something about the danger turned him on even more. And anyway, fuck him, he thought, if he could fuck people in their room then so could he.

"We can go to mine." David said. Tim guy raised an eyebrow and gave a little smirk. "My roommate is out at lectures. We should be fine, might just have to be quick."

The two guys stood staring at each other. Sexual tension ripping between them, filling them both with anticipation. All they wanted to do was fuck and they didn't care where or how it happened.

"It'll be fine. C'mon, let's go" David said and with that the two guys made their way back to David's room.

When they made it back to the room there was a moment of awkward silence as they settled into the quiet of the space. Then, the guy grabbed David's neck and pulled him in close, kissing and biting at his lips.

The kiss deepened quickly and David found himself on the bed with Tim's body pressed on top of him. Hands groped at his skin and fingers dug into his hair as the other boy took hold of David's dick through his jeans. The kiss broke and David stared at him with hooded eyes. He couldn't believe how attractive this guy was, his face lit up, and his eyes burned. David couldn't help himself and reached out to grab his face. Tim responded by deepening the kiss. His hands explored the whole length of David's body and David let him touch him.

David's head swam with ecstasy. He couldn't contain himself. He pulled Tim closer. Tim moaned lightly, a low sexy sound vibrating from his throat, as David held him in place. Both their breathing became unsteady as their tongues danced around each other. They kept moving, grinding and kissing.

David lifted one leg and wrapped it around Tim's waist. David grabbed hold of a handful of his hair and pulled slightly forcing Tim on top of him.

"Mmm" Tim whispered, "David, you taste so sweet." He groaned.

David moaned too, pulling harder onto Tim's hair as he started rubbing his erection against his thigh. He felt Tim squirm and buck forward slightly on David's erection rubbing against him. David let out another moan of ecstasy. He was ready. He was ready to be fucked, right there in his bed.

"Oh fuck yeah" Tim moaned into the crook of his neck, as he pushed David onto his back and climbed down his chest. Tim looked down and started unzipping David's jeans. He fumbled with the zipper, not quite able to pull it all the way down, before he managed to slip it completely down.

David was naked from the waist down, Tim

thrusting between his hips, his jeans still on.

"Fuck me." David said. Then they worked together to unbutton Tim's pants and pull his cock out into the open.

"Do you have lube?" he asked.

David fumbled with the drawer next to his bed before pulling out some lube and a condom. Tim sheathed himself then squirted lube over his cock and gave it a few strokes before lining the tip up to David's puckered asshole.

He groaned and then started to push himself into David's hole. Just as the tip entered David the door to the room opened and Liam walked in. Tim panicked and pulled his cock out, covering himself with his hands.

"Don't mind me boy. Carry on." Liam said, as he stared at David, whose legs were up in the air, his asshole on display. "Don't want to spoil your fun." He winked at the guy.

"Fuck sake." Tim said as he tucked his lubed up cock back into his jeans. Giving David a final glimpse of his abs as he pulled his shirt back down.

"I'm so sorry." David said.

"Don't worry about it." Tim said passive aggressively as he made his way out of the room and slammed the door behind him.

Chapter Seven

Liam and David were in the room alone once again. David laying on the bed with his bottom half still naked and cock still throbbing.

"We need to stop making a habit of this. I keep getting a view of your cock."

David didn't even flinch. He just slay there, staring at Liam, furious and majorly turned on.

"Sorry for cockblocking you again." Liam shrugged as he chucked his bag down and sat on the side of his bed. David was flushed red, his legs splayed, watching Liam's movements carefully.

"It's like you're enjoying it." David said.

Liam paused for a moment and then said, "Maybe I am." and he winked at David again. Listen, don't let me stop you. If you need to finish yourself off, go ahead. I'm not squeamish. Don't want you getting blue balls, I'll never hear the end of it."

David hesitated a moment, not entirely sure what Liam was suggesting. Then he realised. He looked down at his cock, his foreskin half pulled back, the veins gently pushing out his skin. Something snapped in him, and suddenly any shame or embarrassment he felt just disappeared. He brought his right hand to his cock and gently started stroking up and down, his foreskin massaging his bellend as it went over it. Almost like he was doing it to spite Liam.

Liam chuckled to himself, but seemed unfazed by David's wanking in front of him. For a moment he pretended to busy himself with taking stuff out of his bag, then he leant back on his bed and watched David moaning as he stroked his cock up and down.

David's left hand came to his balls as he pulled them down and teased his hole with his fingers. Liam smirked again.

David noticed something that he hadn't expected to see. He saw a bulge growing out of Liam's sweatpants. He was hard. David smirked back at Liam and nodded to Liam's crotch.

"You got me. I can't help it, I get turned on easily. I am a man after all." Liam began rubbing his crotch through his joggers.

"Why don't you join me?" David said as he

continued stroking his cock, the excitement building, his smooth skin reddening from the heat.

Liam smiled and thought for a moment, then slowly pulled the elastic of his pants down. He wasn't wearing any underwear, slowly Liam's neat brown pubes were in sight. Then David saw the base of Liam's shaft, the waistband pulling his cock down as it lowered. Then as the waistband crept past the tip of Liam's cock, it bounced free and slapped against his stomach. Then Liam teased his fingers along the length of it before grabbing it between his fingers and beginning to jerk.

They both lay there, jerking together for a few moments, before Liam stood and kicked his pants off. Then he walked over to David, still stroking himself, a light grunting coming from his mouth.

David had never been more turned on in his life. Liam made it to the edge of David's bed, his cock level with David's head. David took the hint and pushed his mouth down the length of Liam. Taking in the sweet taste of Liam's cock.

Liam lifted his T-shirt off as David continued

bobbing up and down on his dick. His abs were perfectly defined, a slight glaze of sweat dappled across his pecks. Liam grabbed David's hair and pushed his head up and down the length of his dick, grunting with every thrust.

"It's nice to have a little bitch boy as my roommate." Liam said as David choked on his length, his cheeks flushing even redder.

After a few more thrusts Liam grabbed David's cheeks and pulled him off of his cock. Staring into his eyes. Then he sway his hips to smack his dick against David's cheeks, making him whimper with desire.

"I want your dick in me." David said.

Liam smirked then pushed David down and swung him around so his ass was up in the air. Liam standing while David was on all fours his face pressed into the bed.

Liam grabbed David's fat ass cheeks and spread them wide, teasing his cock along David's pursed little hole. David squirmed in delight, moaning.

"Fuck me, please fuck me."

Liam slapped David's ass cheek in response,

earning another wimper from David. Liam's tip fit snuggly between David's cheeks as Liam gently pushed, teasing the hole with his end. Then Liam grabbed his cock and slapped it against the hole a few times, staring with hunger.

"There's lube in the drawer." David said. Liam Slapped his asscheek again then leant over to grab the lube, slathering it up and down his cock and squirting some onto David's asshole, before massaging it into his hole with his index finger. David let out little moans with each thrust of Liam's finger.

When David was lubed and relaxed Liam finally began pushing his length inside David's ass. David's virgin ass was so tight it made Liam groan with pleasure. Liam kept pushing deeper and deeper into David, before finally he was all the way in. When he was fully inside, he paused and threw his head up to the ceiling as he groaned and spread David's cheeks even further apart.

"Oh fuck, that feels so good." David whimpered. "Fuck me, Liam. I'm ready for it."

Liam smacked David's asscheek and then slowly

began pulling his cock in and out of David's ass, grunting with every thrust. Slapping his thighs against David's asscheeks.

"I'm going to fill you to bursting, baby boy." Liam said. David whimpered again and closed his eyes. His body quivering.

Liam's hips were moving faster now, slamming into David's asscheek again and again, making him whimper in pain as he did so.

When David looked back he saw Liam's face full of pleasure as he was pounding him into the bed. Grabbing on to David's t-shirt for leverage.

Fucking him into a pulp. They fucked for what felt like hours, grunting and panting. The pleasure building to extremes for both of them. David had never felt so alive in all his life. He finally knew what it felt like to be fucked and no book could ever replace the feeling of Liam's dick pulsing inside him. He was alive.

David could feel Liam's orgasm coming on. He tried reaching for Liam's hand, but he was too far away. He reached his hand up towards Liam's arm instead and wrapped his fingers around Liam's wrist. It was almost impossible, he barely held onto Liam's wrists as Liam thrusted. He was close. Very close. David could feel his dick twitch within him, ready for release.

David used his other hand to continue pumping his own cock as he was fucked. The friction feeling amazing against his prostate. But he needed one final hit, needed Liam to cum inside him. Just before Liam released he pumped his dick hard enough to make his balls jump. His orgasm rushing to meet Liam. He arched his hips, bucking against Liam, letting loose all the pent up tension. Their sweaty bodies slamming against each other.

David let out a loud moan as the orgasm washed over him, cum squirting from his dick as his ass clenched around Liam's cock, sending him over the edge.

Then Liam grunted louder than ever as his cock was grabbed even tighter in David's ass. David could feel his ass filling with spurt after spurt of Liam's cum. He could feel his body tensing around Liam's cock, could hear the sound of their flesh slapping against each other as Liam slowed his thrusts to a stop.

Liam slumped down over David and kissed his back.

"Fuck, that was good." Liam gasped.

"Really fucking good." David responded.

They were still for a few moments, panting, before Liam began to pull himself out of David. David savoured the sweet pain of every inch of Liam's cock as it left him. When Liam was finally all the way out, David stayed in position, his ass pointing up into the air, his face in the bedsheets. He could feel Liam's cum dripping down from his hole. He had never felt anything so satisfying in all of his life. Liam slapped his cheek again and then collapsed on the bed next to him, pulling him over and into a hug.

"Glad I finally got to cum in your ass. I've been fantasising about that." Liam said.

"You have?" David said as he lay on Liam's chest.

"I told you, I'm a horny fucker. Difficult for me to share a room with someone and not have fantasies. I'd never fucked a guy before, but always thought an asshole would feel amazing and tight to cum inside. I wasn't wrong. That was fucking great." They both chuckled before slowly falling off into a deep and contented sleep

Chapter Eight

The next morning David woke up in the bed, alone. He turned over and scanned his eyes across the room looking for Liam. He was nowhere to be seen.

He sighed and got out of the bed, stretching himself. He was still half naked, his limp dick dangling around between his legs. He made his way over to the window with a knowing smile on his face. Last night was so amazing, he had finally lost his virginity and, even better - he lost it to Liam.

David wondered how Liam was feeling this morning. Did he regret what they had done? Why had he run off without saying anything? David could feel his stomach start to turn slightly with the worry about what it would be like to share a room with Liam from now on. David grabbed his phone to check if he had any messages, but it was completely blank.

He pulled on some underwear and sat on his bed, staring at Liam's stuff on the opposite side of the room. He was getting horny again just thinking about the night before. God it felt good to have Liam inside of him. Cumming inside of him.

Moments later Liam walked back into the room

holding a brown paper bag and two cups of coffee.

"Morning sunshine." Liam said as he shut the door behind him and gave one of his easy smiles to David. "Coffee?"

"I'd love some." David said, sitting up on his bed watching as Liam placed a cup in David's hands.

"So what do you have planned for today?" David asked as he blew at his coffee to cool it down.

"Is that you trying to play it cool?" Liam chuckled.

"Don't tease me! I'm just trying to break the tension."

"Tension? What tension? I had my cock up your ass last night, how much tension can there be between us after that?" Liam laughed and lightly punched David on the arm before taking a seat on his bed, sitting opposite David.

"Don't get all weird about it. I had fun!" Liam said.

"I'm not weird, I just know you've probably not been with a guy before and..."

"No, but I have had my cock inside people before. It's not something weird and abnormal, we were just enjoying each other. Sex is natural and nothing to be ashamed of. But listen, if you're feeling weird about it I'm happy to talk. I know for you it might not just have been a fuck. It's not like I'm your boyfriend now."

"It's fine, I know you're straight and just messing

around. I don't expect anything from you."

"I don't want to be an asshole either though. I get it, sex brings up feelings. We're friends, you can talk to me about anything. Don't play any of that, 'I don't need to talk to anyone, I don't need any help.' bullshit."

David chuckled, he felt his stomach clench with the urge to keep his mouth shut about how he really felt. But looking into Liam's eyes he wondered if it was time to take a risk.

"Well, listen. I am gay and of course at some point I would like a boyfriend. I want to have some romance. But I feel like I don't really know myself at all. I spent my whole childhood with so many rules and feeling like everything I did was wrong. My Dad was a cop you see, so there was no escape for me. And now I'm here, I really want to go mad and experiment and make mistakes, but I can't stop the feeling inside me that I'm just a piece of shit."

"I get that, can't be easy growing up with a cop for a Dad, he must have been crazy strict. My parents were barely around at all, so I had the complete opposite."

"I'm sorry to hear that. But last night really was great, It was the first time I actually let go and allowed myself to do just what I felt. When I started wanking in front of you it was the scariest thing I had ever done. But I've never felt more alive. And listen, I don't want to be your boyfriend. But if you ever want to, y'know, experiment some more. I'm up for it."

Liam chuckled and David thought he caught a slight blush come onto his cheeks.

"Well listen, I'm just finding myself here too. And I don't know what I feel or what I want. But, I really liked fucking you. So, yeah, as long as things won't be too weird. I'm happy to experiment some more with you."

David could feel his cock getting hard at the thought of it. He felt that same old feeling try to shut him down. But then he stared into Liam's eyes, a weird chaotic charm twinkling in them. Then he felt some courage, got to his feet and pulled his t-shirt and underwear off letting his hard cock bounce free into the room. He stood there proudly, completely naked, with his hands on his hips watching Liam's playful expression as he looked at David's cock throbbing.

"Well in that case. If you want me to be honest about how I'm feeling. I could do with a hand right now. I've got some major morning horn." David said.

Liam smirked, put down his coffer and paused for a moment before he beckoned David over with his hand. David walked over with confidence to Liam's bed, then straddled him. Liam placed his hands on David's bare asscheeks and snuck his finger round to David's hole.

"I like this new side of you. I thought I was gonna be stuck with my repressed little roommate for the whole year." Liam said.

"I'm afraid you might have created a monster. You're not the only horny little fucker in here." David smiled as he bit Liam's ear.

"Oh, I bet." Liam whispered as he rocked David back and forth on top of him, rubbing his erection through his clothes. Then Liam lifted David and flipped him onto the bed. David lay with his legs up, exposing his asshole to Liam. Liam ripped his clothes off and then brought his mouth down and he began eating David's asshole as he jerked himself. His tongue causing David to moan and squirm.

The boys were so turned on, they didn't want to waste any time. Liam grabbed the lube from David's bed side table. Slathered his cock yet again and within moments he was inside David, where he belonged. David wrapped his legs around Liam's waist and his arms around Liam's neck. They paused for a moment, staring into each other's eyes, then their tongues met as they consumed each other while Liam began thrusting in and out of David's tight hole.

"I'm yours to fuck whenever you want." David whispered in between kisses.

"I know." Liam grunted as he plunged his cock in and out of David's boy pussy, sweat building yet again all over his body.

He put an arm behind David's neck for more leverage as he quickened his pace. David furiously stroking himself in time to Liam's thrusts. He moaned loudly, his orgasm starting to build. Liam positioned above David, his cock buried inside him, pounding into him harder. The two boys were breathing heavily against each other's skin. David grabbed onto the sheets beneath him tightly as he pushed his head back on the bed to give Liam more access.

Their moans and movements grew louder and more frantic until finally Liam was shooting his load once again deep into David's ass, while David screamed and shot ribbons of hot cum all over his chest.

Their breathing slowed, Liam started to pull out when David grabbed his asscheek.

"Stay inside me. I want all of your cum." David whispered. They stayed for a few moments before Liam removed himself and they cleaned themselves up, awkwardly giggling and smiling to each other.

"I got you some breakfast by the way." Liam said

as he chucked the paper bag in David's direction. "If you are going to be my new fuck toy, I thought I had better treat you right." Liam gave a sweet wink and kissed David on the head.

"Well I'm just happy for the free breakfast." David said as he took a bite of the pastry, letting a satisfied smile spread across his face. "Y'know, I wasn't sure I was going to enjoy my time here. Especially not sharing a room with you." He chuckled, "But I don't know, I can't help but feel this is going to be the best year, ever." David smiled as he lay back on Liam's bed, his body filling with excitement at all the opportunities that lay at his feet. All he had to do, was take them.

I hope you enjoyed the book!
I'm an independent author so your feedback is really valuable. Please leave a review if you can or feel free to drop me some personal feedback to: tomnorthauthor@gmail.com
If you would like to sign-up to my mailing list for offers and news on future releases please follow the link: https://mailchi.mp/1613c8979d1a/tom-north-narratotr
Thanks for reading!
Xx

PS. Please continue reading for a sample of some of my other work.

The Cowboy - Sample

Chapter One

The landscape was moving past on rails. Dry yellow hills were undulating up and down like waves as Samuel stared absentmindedly out of the train window.

He had been thinking about this journey for a long time time. He had been fantasizing for years about getting out on his own. Fantasizing about the feeling of freedom, the elation he would feel when he finally had his own space and the ability to carve his own future.

On his eighteenth birthday he remembered looking into his Dad's drunken eyes.

"Happy fucking birthday son." his Father spat the words at him.

Later that evening he had beaten Samuel to a pulp.

The railway line was new - still being built in a lot of places. A brand new network connecting the country together. Allowing people to travel around and find something new. The land of hope and freedom was opening up even more. Samuel desperately wanted a slice of it.

The railway would give him everything he ever dreamed of. It would open him up to a whole other life. That's what he told himself.

He hadn't really planned properly where he was going to go. He was hoping he could head out west and get a job doing some mining or ranching somewhere. All his friends in New York would talk about how much opportunity there was out west. How people were making fortunes in mining gold.

It was only after years of his father his father's beatings, that he realised he might need to do something to survive.

The blonde of his hair was reflecting the yellow of the sun. The blue of his eyes looked out of place in that dry arid landscape. His features seemed sharper than the others.

Samuel had always been considered the odd one out. He was always the quiet one. But now was his chance to prove that he wasn't the quiet one. He had the power to take control of his life and make something of himself.

The Train began to slow.

Here seemed as good a place as any. This would be his home - for now at least.

He slowly gathered his bag and climbed off of the train feeling the heat of the desert sun hitting him. There weren't many people around. It was midday. The station was a lonely outpost on the outskirts of the town. Goldenbluff it was called. That seemed to make sense.

The station was a small wooden shack with a few windows. Samuel had to walk past a group of rough looking men dressed in ragged clothes, who all stopped talking when they saw the man approaching them. One hollered at Samuel.

"Welcome to Goldenbluff."

Samuel tried to respond confidently, but he stuttered out a barely audible greeting. The men just grunted at him in response and then returned to their conversation.

Samuel kept his eyes on his boots as he made his way into town. He had managed to buy the boots before leaving New York. He knew if nothing else he'd need some good footwear for working out there. The landscape was rough and whatever he found himself doing, it was probably going to be physical.

Once inside he felt better. Goldenbluff was a tiny town with a population of about five thousand people. It wasn't too bad, at least not compared to New York.

But there was one thing that stood out to Samuel about the place. The lack of any real law enforcement.

As he approached the post office a young boy stood outside watching the activity. He wore a dirty white shirt with a faded denim vest over it. His long black hair hung loose over his shoulder.

"Excuse me?" Samuel asked awkwardly as he approached. The boy turned to look at him and gave him a suspicious smile.

"Are you looking for a letter or something?" He asked.

"No, no. I came here to look for a job." Samuel responded.

The boy laughed, "Yeah right! You ain't got a clue what you're doing do ya?"

He was a scruffy looking kid around ten years old. He was leaning on a rotten step leading up to the building, his eyes squinting in the sun, his cheeks brown with dirt and dust.

"Well, I'm new in town. Could you point me in the direction of the saloon?" Samuel said politely.

The boy nodded slightly and gestured toward the street ahead of him, "You don't want to go there though. The miners there are a rough bunch and they don't take kindly to new faces."

"Well where should I go then?"

"If I were you I'd get on the first train out of here. This ain't the type of town to set up a new life in." The boy looked Samuel up and down for a few moments. Samuel began to walk way, when the boy shouted after him, "Listen, my sister Lucy works over there in the market. She might know of something going."

"Thanks." Samuel nodded and set off towards the market.

As Samuel walked he felt increasingly uneasy.

This town was strange. People didn't greet each other normally. They either ignored each other or shouted threats. He could tell that this was different from anything back in New York. It really was different out west.

Hopefully, if this Lucy woman knew of some work, she wouldn't just turn him away. He just hoped he didn't come across the same kind of trouble he had with his father. After all, it wasn't hard to pick up a beating when you were the type of person who didn't fit in easily.

Printed in Great Britain
by Amazon